VESUVIUS POOVIUS

To Jonnus Greenhalghius – K.G.

VESUVIUS POOVIUS
by Kes Gray and Chris Mould

British Library Cataloguing in Publication Data
A catalogue record of this book is available
from the British Library.

ISBN: 0340 87336 1 (PB)

First published in hardback in 2003
This paperback edition first published 2004
10 9 8 7 6 5 4 3 2

Published by Hodder Children's Books,
a division of Hodder Headline Limited,
338 Euston Road, London, NW1 3BH

Originated by Dot Gradations Ltd, UK

Printed in China

VESUVIUS POOVIUS

Written by
Kes Gray

Illustrated by
Chris Mould

Hodder Children's Books

A division of Hodder Headline Limited

IT WAS ANOTHER PONGY DAY IN STINKY ROME.

Soldiers gasped on their way to war.

Children fainted on their way to school.

Everyone hurried on, as fast as they could, trying to get away from the whiff. The whiff of the unmentionable.

(OK, I'll mention it...)

The whiff of poo.

Poo was a big problem in Ancient Rome because no one knew what to do with it.

Some people hid it under the carpet.

Other people dropped it down the well.

Some people even dropped it into other people's pockets when they weren't looking.

Poo was not only a problem in Ancient Rome, it was a FORBIDDENUS WORDUS.

To save his wife's blushes the Emperor had decreed that no one was allowed to say the whiffy word.

"You must think of nicer words to say. Delightful words. Like marzipan or strawberries or jewels. Any citizen of Rome who utters the unmentionable word will be chopped up into little pieces and fed to my dogs."

"I did a huge daffodil last night," said Numerus Twoous.
"I did a couple of quite big honey bees this morning," said Loous Bloous.
"What did you do with yours?" said Numerus Twoous.
"I threw mine over Vesuvius Poovius' fence."
"Me too," said Numerus Twoous. "He'll never notice."

Indeed, Vesuvius Poovius hadn't noticed.
He was far too busy with his slide rule and crayons.
Vesuvius Poovius was a Roman inventor and for many years he had been trying to solve the problem of unmentionables.

He had tried the stomping effect. But flatter and wider was no solution at all. He had tried the catapult principle. But that only lobbed the problem somewhere else.

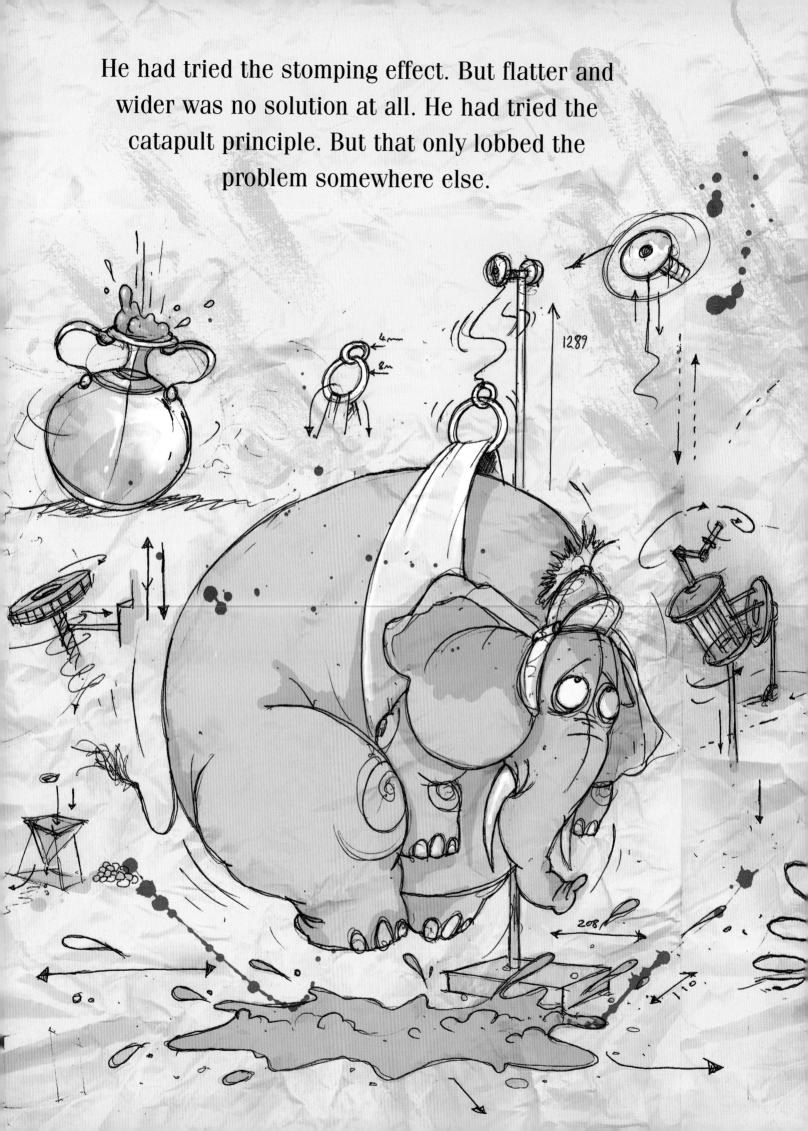

Vesuvius Poovius had tried all sorts of things, but now for the first time he really believed he was on to something. A new idea had come to him the night before…

He was lying in bed listening to the rain and wondering how moles disposed of their jelly beans, when a lightning flash lit up the sky. Vesuvius sat up and stared at the rain.

"Tunnels!"
he cried.

"Tunnels and rain! That's it!

I will build a system of tunnels beneath Rome and I will build a rainwater flushing system for flushing away the unmentionables!"

It wasn't just clever. It was Vesuvius Poovius Genius! He wrote a letter to the Emperor straight away.

Dear Emperor,

I bring great news. After many years of examining the problem of daffodils I am pleased to tell you that I have cracked it! Sugar lumps, fairy cakes and custard creams will no longer be the curse of Ancient Rome.

I have designed a new jam tart disposal system. It can dispose of rose buds, budgerigars, nightingales and even chocolate custard.

You must come and see it, even better come and try it!

Vesuvius read the letter back to himself and then screwed it up. It didn't make one jot of sense. If the Emperor read it he'd probably be arrested and thrown into prison for being mad. He might even end up as dog food.

He needed a different plan. He sucked his pen, thought very hard and wrote another letter. This time it was very short, but very clever.

Vesuvius read the letter to himself and smiled. Two good ideas in one night. "I'm on a roll!"

Dear Mr and Mrs Emperor,

Please come to my birthday party on Tuesday.

IV till VI

Love

Vesuvius Unmentionablevius

All week, Vesuvius busied
himself preparing
for the visit of the
Emperor and
his wife.

He was just blowing up the
last party balloon when he heard
a loud knock on his door.

Vesuvius looked at his sundial.
"IV o'clock already! The Emperor
and his wife are here!"

The Emperor and his wife strode in wearing golden party hats.
"Happy Birthday, Vesuvius!" they cried.
"Where's the party tea?"
Vesuvius pointed to the lounge.
"Tuck in!" he smiled. "There's prune cocktail,
sheep's eye dumplings, eel jelly, frog burgers,
beetle pizza, snail squash, crow soup
and lots, lots more!"

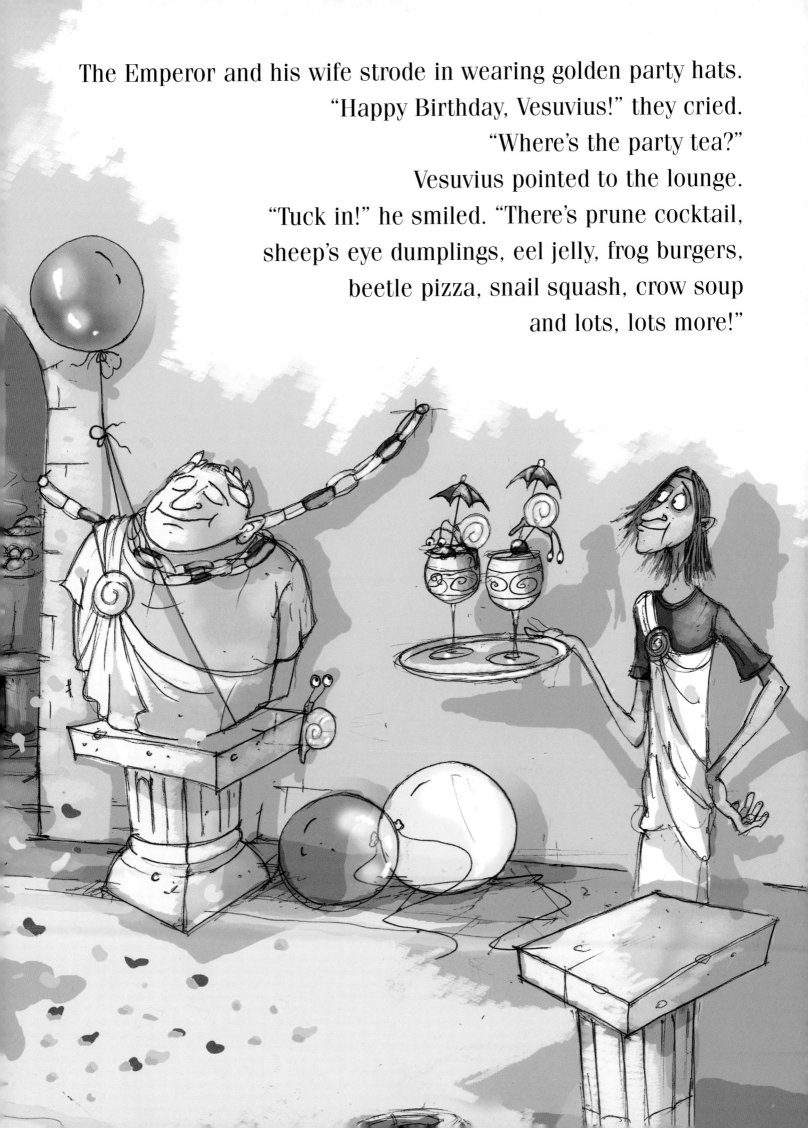

The Emperor and his wife loved a good feast
and dived in straight away.

"Not hungry, Vesuvius?" said the Emperor,
with a mouthful of jelly fish crisps.
"Not really," said Vesuvius with a shudder.

"These sugared snails are delicious,"
grunted the Emperor's wife.
"This is my fourteenth!"

Munch by munch, slurp by slurp and belch by belch,
the Emperor and his wife worked their way through
the tummy curdling lot.

Finally,
with a burp and
a grunt they flopped out on the sofa in a heap.
"Vesuvius," said the Emperor, "that was
the finest party tea I've ever had!"
"Yes," said the Emperor's wife with a
belch. "Such a nice change from hens'
beaks in breadcrumbs."

"I'm pleased you enjoyed it," said Vesuvius. "Can I get you something else? There's honeyed hedgehogs in the larder."

The Emperor raised his thumb, but then shifted slightly in his seat. He lowered his hand and placed it on his huge balloon of a belly. "On second thoughts, Vesuvius, I think I'll pass."

"Not for me, either," said the Emperor's wife, who had begun to look rather green.

The Emperor's tummy gurgled loudly.
He nudged his wife.
"I think I'm going to explode,"
he whispered.
"Me too," she squeaked.
"Would you like an after dinner
sheep's eye?" asked Vesuvius
mischievously.
The Emperor squirmed.
"Some squid ink tea perhaps?"
smiled Vesuvius.
The Emperor's wife wriggled
uncomfortably.
"We really couldn't,"
she gasped.

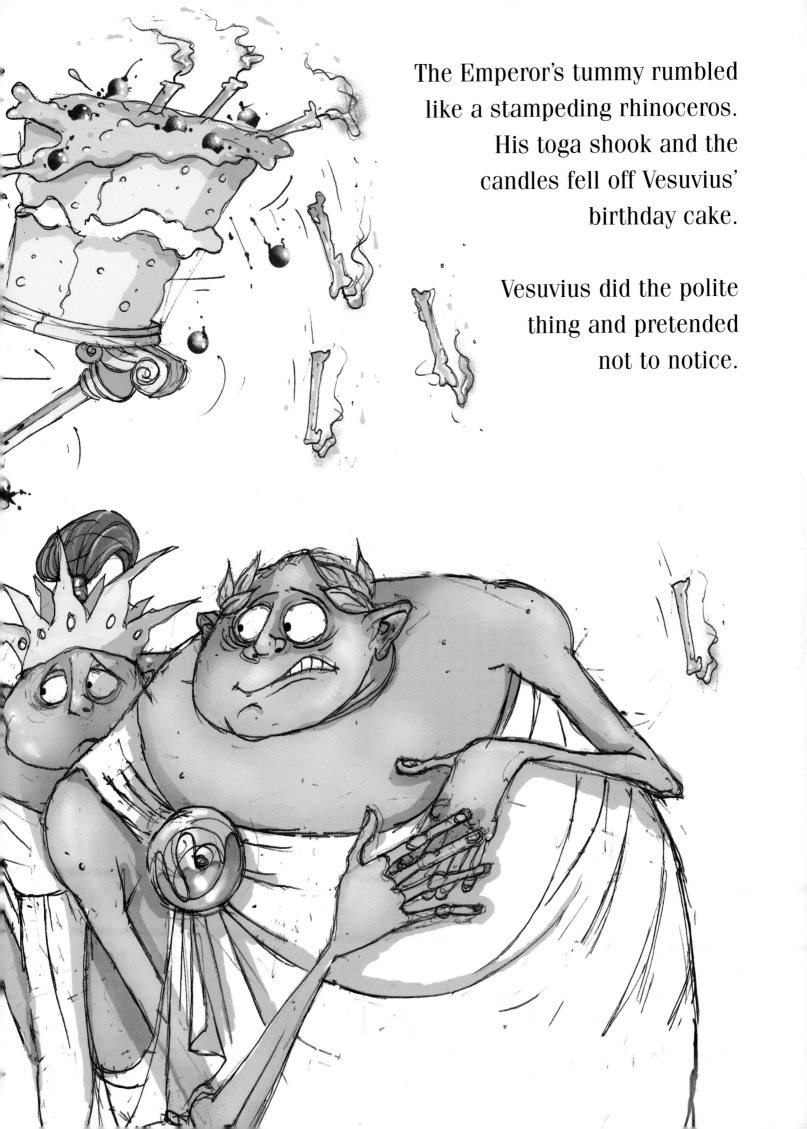

The Emperor's tummy rumbled like a stampeding rhinoceros. His toga shook and the candles fell off Vesuvius' birthday cake.

Vesuvius did the polite thing and pretended not to notice.

The Emperor's wife's tummy gurgled like a blocked drain. She placed both hands under her bottom and squirmed like an eel. She wasn't green any more, she was white. Her eyes were bulging and her lips were pinched tight. Her husband placed a cushion over his belly as another thunderous rumble shook a mosaic from the wall.

The Emperor's ears began to throb and
his bottom began to tremble.
"Vesuvius," he groaned.
"I'm awfully sorry,
but I very much need to do…
We positively have to do…
"A cola cube," squealed his wife.
"A sugar mouse," gasped the Emperor.

Vesuvius smiled politely.
"I'm sorry, I don't understand," he said.
The Emperor and his wife leapt up from the sofa.

"A POO! Vesuvius!" screamed the Emperor.
"WE NEED TO DO A POO!!!"

"Quick, follow me!" said Vesuvius.
The Emperor and his wife dashed out of the lounge
and followed Vesuvius down the hallway.

"Use these," said Vesuvius, pointing
to two gleaming marble seats.
The Emperor and his wife were in too much
of a hurry to ask questions.

They lifted up their togas and dived for the seats…

Vesuvius went back to the lounge to clear up the party plates.
He was halfway through the washing-up when the Emperor
and his wife bounced into the kitchen
and slapped him on the back.

"VESUVIUS!
YOUR INVENTION!
IT'S MARVELLUS!
IT'S FABULUS!
IT'S INCREDIBLUS!
WHAT IS IT?"

"I have called it the Vesuvius Poovius Loovius, or 'Loo'
for short," he smiled.
"Get the honeyed hedgehogs out!" said the Emperor.
"And the squid ink tea!" said his wife. "We want to have
another go!"

And go and go they did.

The next day, the Emperor decreed that every villa in Rome was to be fitted with Vesuvius' new invention.

Vesuvius became a national hero. His birthday became a Roman holiday and everywhere he went he was carried shoulder high. In fact, even today, some people still leave their loo seats up as a salute to Vesuvius Poovius.